Published in 2021 by Groundwood Books / House of Anansi Press
groundwoodbooks.com

Groundwood Books respectfully acknowledges that the land on which we operate is the Traditional Territory of many Nations, including the Anishinabeg, the Wendat and the Haudenosaunee. It is also the Treaty Lands of the Mississaugas of the Credit.

We gratefully acknowledge for their financial support of our publishing program the Canada Council for the Arts, the Ontario Arts Council and the Government of Canada. Nathalie Dion thanks the Conseil des arts et des lettres du Québec for its financial support.

Canada Council
for the Arts

Conseil des Arts
du Canada

ONTARIO ARTS COUNCIL
CONSEIL DES ARTS DE L'ONTARIO
an Ontario government agency
un organisme du gouvernement de l'Ontario

With the participation of the Government of Canada
Avec la participation du gouvernement du Canada | Canadä

Conseil
des arts
et des lettres
du Québec

Library and Archives Canada Cataloguing in Publication
Title: My mad hair day / Nathalie Dion.
Names: Dion, Nathalie, author, illustrator.
Identifiers: Canadiana (print) 20200394320 | Canadiana (ebook) 20200394339 | ISBN 9781773065113 (hardcover) | ISBN 9781773065120 (EPUB) | ISBN 9781773065137 (Kindle)
Classification: LCC PS8607.I6445 M9 2021 | DDC jC813/.6—dc23

The illustrations in this book were created with a mix of digital and watercolor painting.

Printed and bound in China

MIX
Paper from
responsible sources
FSC® C144853

To (late) Odette for the momentum to write,
to France for the falling piano and to Karen Li
for her precious contribution to this tall tale.

MY MAD HAIR DAY

Nathalie Dion

Groundwood Books / House of Anansi Press

Toronto / Berkeley

My name is Malie
and I H-A-T-E my curly hair!
This morning when I woke up it was wilder
than ever.
It was a huge tangled mess!

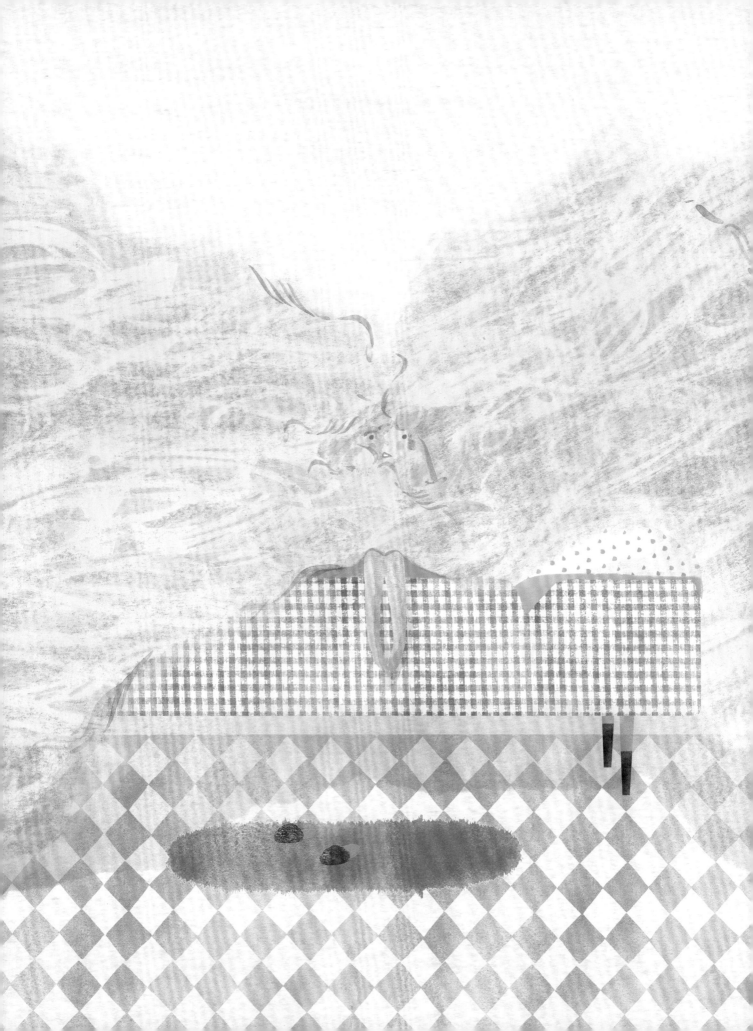

I tried to comb it

and hide it under a cap.

Poof!

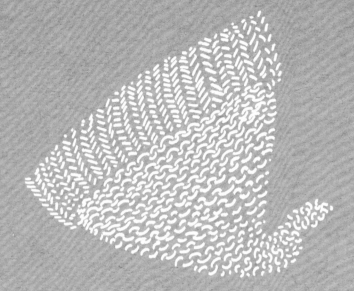

Nothing worked.

I wanted to lock myself inside
and never come out again.

But Mama had other plans.

She gave me a list of errands to run, which
forced me from my cozy closet.
I left in a huff.

As I stepped out, the wind picked up.

Even worse, rain started to fall before
I could get to the bus shelter.
Believe it or not, my hair became
even *hairier*!

At the baker's, my big hair swept all
the cupcakes off a silver tray.

A flock of birds, drawn to
my irresistible nest, made it
their home.

A lost lamb thought he'd found
his mother and curled up inside
my curls.

When I passed by the barber shop,
I came within a whisker of having it
all shaved off.

When the barber's neighbor,
a frustrated musician,
pushed his grand piano out
the window, it landed ...

Can you guess where?

A tricyclist slipped and flipped but
enjoyed the softest landing ...

You can guess where.

It was all too much to bear!

So I gave myself a time-out.